The Fairies, hiding in-between
the layers of nature's mysteries,
wish to thank everyone
who cherishes and
respects our environment.

Fairy Flight

by Tracy Kane

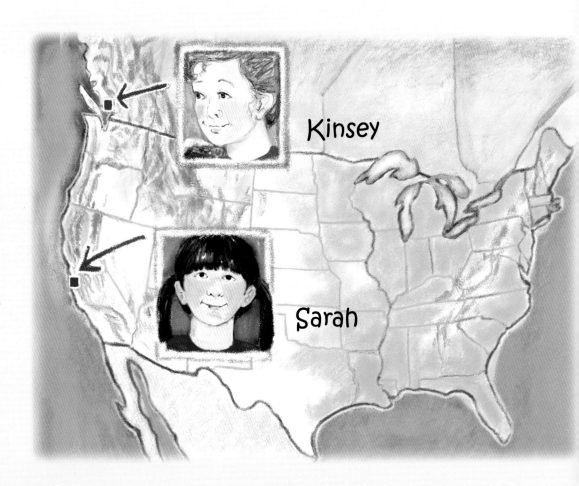

Kinsey had waited all year for her cousin Sarah to come back and visit her in Canada.

Sarah's family had moved from Canada to California last year, and both girls had been counting the days until they would see each other again.

Finally, they were together again ...
and enjoying every moment!

Sarah and Kinsey spent the last lazy days of summer building fairy houses in a meadow near Kinsey's backyard. They gathered natural materials and built enchanting, almost hidden habitats that blended into the landscape.

They called their village "Fairyland."

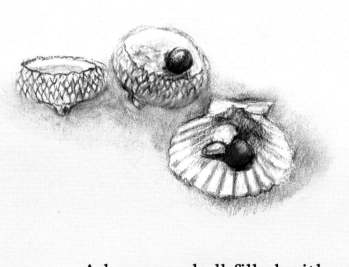

Both girls discovered that acorn caps and small shells were the perfect size for dishes.

A large seashell filled with water made a fairy bathtub.

Kinsey found that dry milkweed pods with their fluffy seeds made lovely soft beds for sleepy fairies.

Sarah showed Kinsey how empty milkweed pods could become little fairy boats. Before launching several in a nearby creek, the girls placed special treats in them for the fairies.

As the boats floated gently in the breeze, a group of butterflies appeared, circled and landed on them. The girls were delighted as the butterflies enjoyed a boat ride!

One curious butterfly landed on Sarah's hand. She whispered to her cousin, "These must be the Monarch butterflies that migrate all the way to my town in California! ...

It's like someone famous is coming. Every year, when they arrive in October, the whole town welcomes them back with a Butterfly Parade."

"Look!" Sarah exclaimed. "This caterpillar will become a Monarch.
Soon it will spin a chrysalis on the milkweed. Last year at school we raised them
and watched as they turned into butterflies."

Kinsey wanted Sarah to show her how to raise them.

So together they searched and found six caterpillars to take home. They gathered extra milkweed to feed the caterpillars and made a home for them in Kinsey's unused fish aquarium.

On the last night of
Sarah's visit, the girls
played music and invented
a fairy dance, spinning each
other around the room
until they were giddy!

The music floated through the room as light glowed mysteriously in the aquarium. The girls felt the night's enchantment, while the caterpillars slept snugly in their newly spun chrysalises.

"I believe butterflies
are really fairies in disguise,"
whispered Kinsey.
"I think the fairies visit at night
and sprinkle fairy dust on the caterpillars ...

and this magic helps change them into butterflies."

After Sarah returned to California, Kinsey began painting a detailed picture of a changing chrysalis to send to her. But suddenly her cat leaped across the table and knocked over a jar.

Blue paint splattered everywhere!
Kinsey gasped as blue droplets
landed on the chrysalises!

She hoped the paint hadn't
hurt the butterflies inside.

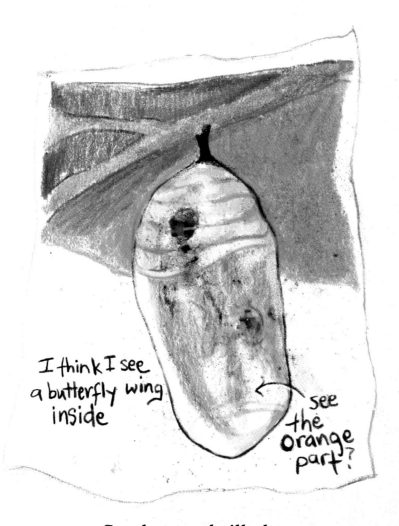

Sarah was thrilled to
receive Kinsey's picture.

Sarah wrote back, sending a drawing of her own.
She was excited because her class would
be marching in the Butterfly Parade.

Several days later, the butterflies emerged
from their chrysalises, dried their wings
and began to fly.

Kinsey realized her butterflies
were different looking from
other Monarch butterflies ...
but they were healthy,
so she released them.

She watched them happily
flitting from flower to flower.

Soon, they joined several other Monarchs
and headed off towards the sunset.

Kinsey waved goodbye, then quickly
ran inside to write Sarah that
their butterflies were
headed her way!

Dad
showed me this
XXO Kinsey ↓

Butterflies take a Balloon Ride

As the sun rose over the Annual Northern California Hot-Air Balloon Festival, thousands of Monarch butterflies appeared. The sky was a rainbow of colors as the butterflies circled and landed on the floating balloons, delighting the people on board and below.

Dear Kinsey,
They're getting close. The Monarchs have been sighted at San Francisco Zoo! I think the fairies guided them there to visit the animals and ride the Merry-go-round! ♡ S

Hi Kinsey,

After the parade I went with my parents to one of the parks where the Monarchs seem to like the trees. Our town protects these places for them. They cuddle close together on the branches and stay sleepy until spring. That's when they begin to fly back to you.

Love Sarah

_____

Make the
Fairies happy
by naming
them!

_____

_____

Visit our website
www.fairyhouses.com